Old Neb and the Lighthouse Treasure

Lois Swoboda

Illustrations by Leslie Wallace-Coon

Pineapple Press, Inc.
Sarasota, Florida

This book is dedicated to Snooky Barber, who told me
the story of Old Neb; to my mother, who will never read it;
to my brother Joe, whom I miss every day of my life;
and to my grandfathers Otto Swoboda and Elmer Metzger,
who taught me everything I really need to know.

Inquiries should be addressed to:
Pineapple Press, Inc.
P.O. Box 3889
Sarasota, Florida 34230

www.pineapplepress.com

Library of Congress Cataloging-in-Publication Data

Swoboda, Lois Elizabeth.
    Old Neb and the lighthouse treasure / Lois Swoboda. — First edition.
        pages cm
    Summary: "Betty spends her summers on St. George Island, where her father is the lighthouse
keeper. Along with her brother Walter, their friend Snooky, and Neb, the lighthouse horse, Betty
embarks on an adventure that leads to treasure."—Provided by publisher.
        ISBN 978-1-56164-787-3 (pbk. : alk. paper)
    1. Saint George Island (Fla.) —Juvenile fiction. I. Title.
        PZ7.1.S96Ol 2015
        [Fic]—dc23

2015001149

Design by Doris Halle
Printed and bound in the USA

Chapter 1

SUMMER had arrived. I couldn't wait to play in the surf, pick blackberries, and chase fireflies. There would be no school and no shoes and I could see Papa everyday. I couldn't wait to ride Old Neb.

My first day back on St. George Island, I woke up before the sunlight came through my window. I'm not sure if it was the sound of the waves and the shorebirds that got my attention or the smell of the ocean or the hum of the bees on the rosemary outside my window, but I was wide awake the instant my eyes popped open. I scooted from between my tangle of sheets and ran to the open window to look outside.

My name is Elizabeth Ann Register, but everybody calls me Betty and my daddy is a lighthouse keeper. I turned eleven in January. In the winter, I go to school on the mainland, in Apalachicola, but my family spends holidays and the summer with Papa, who lives on St. George Island.

That morning, the eastern sky was painted all pink and lavender gold by the sliver of sun peeking over the horizon though it was still night under the tall pine trees. Three deer were quietly grazing on the sea oats at the crest of the dunes.

Silently, so as not to wake up my sister Evelyn, I wriggled into my overalls and stole from my room to the front porch, where I climbed into the porch swing and sat staring at the lighthouse and the morning stealing across the Gulf of Mexico.

Lighthouse keepers work until late at night keeping the beacons lit to guide ships safely to harbor, so I try to keep quiet in the early morning.

I sat curled up on the seat of the big green swing and watched a flight of black skimmers sail in formation just above the bright white and lavender water, with their long lower beaks trailing along the surface to scoop up little fish and other floating things they eat.

The screened door creaked and my brother Walter stepped out onto the porch rubbing his eyes. He looked up and down the beach before climbing up on the swing next to me.

A big pod of dolphins came into view, their black fins bobbing up and down as they meandered along parallel to the shore. They boiled around like popcorn popping, as if they had nowhere in particular to go, which, being dolphins, I guess they didn't.

Walter was eating a cold biscuit left over from last night's supper and he offered me half, which I was happy to take. Mama makes the best biscuits. Papa said it is because she has a very light hand with them. They are still fluffy even when they are cold.

I was licking the last of the crumbs off my fingers when Joseph Proctor, who everybody called Snooky, came tearing around the corner of the house and up onto the porch. The Proctors are our only neighbors on the island. They live on the bay side and we live on the beach by the lighthouse. Snooky is almost eleven and he thinks Walter hung the moon. He spends more time at our house than he does at home.

"Walter," Snooky shouted, "wanna go fishing?"

"Hush, Snooky," said Walter, holding up a hand. "Mama and Papa are still asleep."

Snooky clamped his hands over his mouth and sat down on the porch facing us.

I heard a *clump, clump, clump* and Old Neb came trudging along around the corner following Snooky.

Old Neb is a big horse, as high at the shoulder as I am tall. He has shaggy reddish fur that is not as shiny as the coats of Papa's saddle horses but softer to the touch. He smells like salt water, warm blankets, and horse sweat, which is a smell I like. His nose is soft, fuzzy with stubble like Papa's cheeks before he shaves. I give Neb penny candy and apples and he nuzzles up to the back of my neck and blows through his big warm lips to make me laugh. Neb has big yellow teeth and enormous brown eyes. The only white on him is a little patch on his chest and rings of white fur around his ankles that look like droopy socks.

Neb is the last one of a small herd of horses that had belonged to Mr. Herbert Marshall, who leased part of the island and had grand schemes to make money from it.

One time, Mr. Herbert released some steers out here. I expect he wanted to have the horses available for his cowboys, since his plan was to turn the island into a cattle ranch. Anyway, he turned Neb's family loose on the island to fend for themselves. Mr. Herbert hoped the cattle would thrive on their own and multiply without much help from him. He quickly discovered there was not enough food on St. George for a big cow herd and that ranching was hard work. He gave up on the cattle and sold them, but the horses remained for years, finally dwindling down to Neb, the last survivor of the ranch.

Old Neb works for the lighthouse. He was there to meet our boat last night when we arrived at government dock to spend the summer. Neb hauled us, our luggage, and a month's supply of groceries across the island to the keeper's house in the green buckboard wagon that belongs to the lighthouse.

When we reached home, I gave him a piece of penny candy and he snuffled when he sucked it gently from my hand. Then he went home to his old open-sided shed by the bay where he generally spends his evenings. Mama said he grew up there with his mother and he likes it better than the fancy barn with fly screens the Lighthouse Service built for Papa's saddle horses.

I told Mama I was too excited to sleep last night, but she said we needed to go straight to bed. I guess she was right because I couldn't even remember falling asleep and now it was morning.

I ran to hug Neb and he lowered his head so I could scratch behind his ears.

I turned around to see that Snooky had taken my place on the swing.

"I want to go fishing too," I told the boys.

"I guess you can come," said Walter grudgingly, "but you have to bait your own hook."

"I ain't never been afraid of worms," I said.

Neb pushed his nose against the back of my neck and snuffled. I turned back to him and stroked his forehead.

"I thought you'd never get here," Snooky told Walter, adjusting a ragged straw hat over his mane of thick red hair. "We been here near a week."

"We went to see Mama's sister in Port St. Joe the first week after school let out," I told him. "It was a family obligation."

A delicious smell drifted through the screen door from the general direction of the kitchen and my stomach began to grumble.

"Mama's up," I said.

The three of us walked as quietly as we were able along the wide porch that surrounded the house on all four sides and opened the screen door to the kitchen.

Neb followed us, walking alongside in the sand, and watched with interest when we went inside.

Mama had built up the fire and a cast iron skillet with thick slices of bacon was sizzling and popping on the iron stove. She was cutting slices of white bread and there was butter in a glass-covered dish on the scrubbed wooden table and a jar of blackberry jelly.

Walter and I climbed onto chairs but Snooky lingered just inside the door until Mama looked at him and smiled. He had removed his straw hat and held it in front of him.

"Have you had breakfast, Snooky?" she asked.

"Yes, ma'am, but I could eat again," said Snooky.

"Well, if you three will go and fetch me some eggs, we'll have plenty for everyone," Mama said.

"Can I have something for Neb?" I asked.

Mama frowned.

"Give him the crust of the bread," she said.

I grabbed it and poured on a little of the jam before rolling it into a tube.

Walter and I jumped up and, with Snooky, we scrambled out the door and headed toward the henhouse back by the barn.

I stopped to offer Neb my gift, which he sucked down without chewing like a Hoover vacuum cleaner.

He snorted a thank you and all four of us headed to the henhouse with Neb bringing up the rear.

Walter grabbed up a stick and swung it like a bat as we crossed the yard. Then Snooky had to look for a stick so he could practice batting too. I reached the chicken pen first and propped open the gate to let the chickens scratch in the yard. Mama says chickens chase away snakes.

I entered the henhouse through the low door. The smell was sharp and earthy. Along the walls was a double row of wooden boxes stuffed with hay. Brown, white, and speckled hens were snuggled down in the boxes. I went from nest to nest looking for eggs, sometimes burrowing my hand into the warm, soft straw under a hen to check. When my hands were full, I yelled for Walter and Snooky to come help.

When they finally stuck their heads in the door, my seven-year-old brother Cap'n was with them. I handed off eggs to Walter and Snooky. Cap'n held out his hands too.

"Be careful, Cap'n," I told him, putting an egg in each hand. I watched as he scampered off after the bigger boys. I finished my search, returning to the kitchen with half a dozen speckled brown eggs cradled against my bib overalls.

The breakfast table was set with the basket of homemade bread, sliced tomatoes, and a plate of thick, chewy bacon. There was also a big glass pitcher of fresh, cold milk.

My sister Evelyn was setting out plates, forks, glasses, and butter knives.

Mama broke the eggs into the skillet where she had fried the bacon and they sizzled in the hot grease.

Papa walked in wearing a blue shirt and gray trousers with suspenders hanging down loose around his waist. Beside him padded his dog Trixie. When Papa sat, she lay down at his feet and gazed at us silently with curious ice-blue eyes.

Papa buttered a slice of bread and broke it in half. He offered one piece to Trixie and spread the other with blackberry jam. When Mama poured him coffee, he grabbed her sleeve and kissed her on the cheek. She shooed him away playfully.

"It's good to have you back," he said smiling broadly. "Snooky, how are things at the Proctor house? Settling in well?"

"Yes, sir," said Snooky. "Daddy is coming on Friday to spend the weekend."

"You tell him I'm looking forward to a game of dominoes on Sunday afternoon," said Papa.

"Yes, sir," said Snooky gravely.

"Serve yourselves before it gets cold," said Mama, distributing the eggs straight from the skillet and putting the last one on a saucer for Trixie.

"Can we go fishing?" Walter asked Papa.

"Ask your mother," he replied.

"I had hoped you might help me get some oysters this morning," she said. "I need you to hook Old Neb up to the wagon."

"Okay," said Walter. "I can harness him up for you."

"I can too," I said. "And I'm older."

"Finish your breakfast," Mama said. "Snooky and Walter can harness Neb while Betty helps me wash the dishes."

"No," I said. "It's not fair!"

"It's your turn," said Mama.

"But . . ."

"Listen to your mother," said Papa. "Walter will take his turn tonight."

Walter and Snooky bolted from the table and were about to race through the door when Papa barked, "Snooky!"

Snooky froze in his tracks and spun around.

"I see half a glass of milk by your plate," said Papa. "There's plenty of folks today that don't have enough to eat. We don't waste food here."

Snooky reddened and walked back to the table.

"Yes, sir," he said and gulped down a huge mouthful of milk.

"Would you hurry up," whined Walter.

"Walter, if you can't behave like a civilized person, you can come back to the table and sit until he finishes," said Mama.

"I'm finished," said Snooky wiping a white moustache from his upper lip with the back of his hand.

"Can we go now?" begged Walter.

"Put your plates in the sink," said Papa.

Walter grabbed his glass and plate and practically flung them in the sink. Snooky followed with the rest of their dishes while my brother waited impatiently by the door.

"Now can we go?" begged Walter.

"Yes," said Mama. "Watch out for snakes."

"We will," said Snooky over his shoulder as he followed my brother across the porch.

I took another sip of cold milk and stared glumly at my plate.

"If you're finished, you can start the dishes," said Mama.

I swallowed the last of my milk and set to work. Mama had already put a kettle of water on the stove to heat. I pumped cold water into the sink from the cistern and added the hot water from the kettle along with powdered dish soap.

Papa finished his breakfast and brought me his plate. Then he hitched up his suspenders and went to fetch his boots while I cleared Evelyn's plate and Mama's and set to work.

As I was drying my hands on the dishtowel Mama took a custard, made with the morning's fresh eggs, from the oven and set it on the windowsill to cool.

"We can have that after dinner," she said, more to herself than me.

I heard the boys giggling and talking in the yard.

I ran out onto the porch, banging the door behind me.

Snooky and Walter were approaching the house, riding in the buckboard wagon with Walter holding Old Neb's reins.

Cap'n and my sister Evelyn, who is six, were playing with wooden blocks on the porch.

When Mama came outside, she was carrying a basket over her arm and a blue metal stew pot with a lid. She wore a broad-brimmed straw hat.

"Walter, you stay with Cap'n and Evelyn while Betty and I go oyster hogging," said Mama.

"But I want to go!" said Walter.

Snooky just looked stunned.

"Hop down, boys. Betty, you put on your boots and take the reins," Mama said as she pulled on a pair of black rubber boots standing by the kitchen door.

I shoved my bare feet into yellow boots, which stood on the porch next to Mama's, and danced to the buckboard. I scrambled up onto the seat and took the reins from my brother, who gave me an evil look as he climbed from the wagon.

"Walter, fetch me the milking stool from the barn and put it in the wagon," Mama said.

Walter kicked the sand.

"Scoot!" said Mama.

He raced off towards the barn, followed by Snooky, and in short order they returned with Snooky carrying a three-legged wooden stool atop his head.

Mama took it and put it in the back of the wagon.

She climbed up onto the seat beside me and pulled a pink sunbonnet from the pocket of her apron.

"Put it on," said Mama.

"But I don't need . . ." I began.

Mama shushed me. "You are growing into a young lady and I won't have you looking like a wild Indian. I want you to keep the sun off your face."

"But Mama!"

"Put on your bonnet," said Walter, patting at his hair with his fingertips. Snooky was trying to conceal his laughter behind the palm of his hand but it leaked out around the edges.

"You two simmer down or I'll take a switch to you," said Mama. "Put it on," she told me.

I pulled the hat over my hair and Mama fixed the ribbon under my chin in a bow.

"Now you stay with Cap'n and sister until I get back," Mama told Walter.

Walter and Snooky climbed on the swing and sat side by side, frowning, with their arms crossed in front of them.

"Let's go or we'll miss the low tide," said Mama.

I flicked the reins and Neb set off for the bay. He always seemed to know where we were going without being told.

I could feel the boys' eyes boring into my back as we rode away and I heard Walter guffaw as we crossed the dunes.

We set out across the island on a wide sandy path under a canopy of green pines.

Mama began to hum "Leaning on the Everlasting Arms" and I sang along.

Chapter 2

SINCE it was still early morning, it was tolerably cool and a fresh breeze off the Gulf kept the flies away.

"I know you don't understand yet," said Mama, "but you will soon be of an age when boys will look different to you and you will want to look nice for them. That's why I want you to start wearing a bonnet when you're in the sun. A young lady should protect her skin."

"I don't want to be a young lady," I said. "I want to be a pilot like Amelia Earhart."

"Well, where did that come from?" asked Mama, smiling sideways at me.

"I read about her in the paper," I said. "She flew across the Atlantic Ocean. She doesn't care about boys."

"Amelia Earhart is married," said Mama, "so she must think about them a little. You keep your bonnet on."

"She's married?" I demanded.

"Yes," said Mama.

"Walter doesn't have to wear a bonnet."

"You keep your bonnet on and let me worry about Walter," said Mama.

By this time, we had reached the clearing on the bay side of the island and the Proctor house that stood by government dock.

"Stay here," said Mama. She climbed from her seat and headed for the house calling, "Dora! Dora!"

Mrs. Dora Proctor walked out onto the porch, wiping her hands on a yellow gingham apron. She was a tiny woman with pale skin, gooseberry green eyes, and red hair coiled into a bun at the base of her neck. Her two little girls, Dooley and Honey, hung behind in the doorway staring at us with eyes the color of a blue jay's jacket.

"Rachel! Good morning," Miss Dora said. "I'm so happy to see you! And good morning to you too, Betty," she said, nodding in my direction. "You look very fetching in your bonnet."

I hung my head.

"Good morning, Dora," said Mama. "Betty, what do you say?"

"Good morning, Miss Dora," I mumbled.

Mama and Miss Dora hugged.

"Won't you come in for coffee?" asked Miss Dora.

"No, I'm going hogging and wanted to know if you would like a mess of oysters," Mama told her.

"Well, that's kind," said Miss Dora. "Yes, I would. Do you want me to send Butch along to help?"

"Oh, no, I think we can manage," said Mama quickly.

"I can't find him anyway," said Miss Dora and she commenced to calling for her oldest boy, Butch, who was nearly fourteen.

Eventually, Butch shambled around the corner of the house on feet too big for his skinny legs. He stood beside the porch with big ungainly hands crammed in the pockets of raggedy cut-off dungarees. He wore no shirt or shoes and his sun-bleached hair looked like a squirrel's nest.

Neb eyed him suspiciously.

"Where have you been?" asked Miss Dora. "You haven't even washed your face or run a comb through your hair this morning, have you?"

"Aw, Ma . . ." grumbled Butch.

"Looking like that in front of company too!"

Butch slouched even more.

"They ain't company," he muttered.

"Don't you disagree with me," snapped Miss Dora. "You go over to the shed and fetch a basket for Miss Rachel. She's going to carry us some oysters. Hurry up now!"

Butch shuffled off in the direction of the shed.

"I don't know what I am going to do with that boy. I've got a good mind to send him into town to stay with his father, but then he'd be alone during the day and I don't want to think what kind of mischief he'd get up to."

"He's just a boy," said Mama.

She looked down at Honey and Dooley, who had stealthily made their way across the porch to hide behind Miss Dora's skirt.

"I left him to watch my girls last night while I went to the garden to pick some squash. He told them ghost stories and then, after I put them to bed, he put a sheet over his head and scratched at their window! I thought I'd never get them to sleep and he dirtied the sheet up! I had just taken it in off the line."

"Well, I expect Butch gets a little bored. He's at that age, you know," said Mama "How are you angels this morning?" she asked the little girls.

Neither one of the skinny little towheads replied. They buried their faces deep in Miss Dora's flowered cotton skirt.

"Honey, Dooley, don't be rude. Miss Rachel spoke to you."

"Good mornin', Miss Rachel," they squeaked, although Dooley, the younger sister, squeaked it through the skirt.

"That's better," said Miss Dora and she absently placed a hand on each white blond head as she stared unhappily in the direction of the shed.

"Butch!" she shouted so suddenly it made Mama jump.

Old Neb snorted and pawed the ground as if anxious to resume our ride. He looked at me over his shoulder with the whites showing all the way around the brown center of his big eyes.

"Hush now, Neb," I told him, tugging a little on the reins.

"Where is that boy?" fretted Miss Dora.

Neb swung his head in the direction of the shed as if he wondered where Butch was too.

"I'm sure he'll be right along," said Mama, straightening the bodice of her dress. "You look like you've been cooking this morning."

Miss Dora looked at her apron and bundled it up as if to hide it.

"The satsumas already have ripe fruit. I was putting by marmalade. I'll bring you some on Sunday, if we're having lunch."

"Of course we are. Snooky told us Frank is coming over for the weekend," said Mama.

"Oh, yes," said Miss Dora, brightening a little. Then she bellowed, "Butch!" in a voice that seemed too big for such a little woman.

Butch emerged from the shed dragging a bushel basket by the handle and carrying a cotton casting net slung over his shoulder.

"Pick it up," said Miss Dora. "You'll tear the bottom off."

Butch put the basket into the wagon.

"I'm going fishing," he said abruptly.

"All right," said Miss Dora, "but come home in time for dinner. And I want you to shuck oysters for supper this afternoon."

Butch shrugged crookedly and wandered off along the path to the lighthouse.

"Let's go, missy," said Mama, climbing back into the wagon.

I clucked my tongue and shook the reins and Neb shuffled off toward the oyster bar. He knew the way by heart. We rode along the beach under clear blue skies. The tide was low and in the shallow places, fingers of mud littered with oyster shell slithered out from the shore. Small clusters of oysters sprouted from the mud here and there, looking like stone roses.

There were holes in the mud that spouted bubbles or seeped water and hermit crabs scuttled across the slick surface in a wide variety of shells ranging from pea-size to as big as a baseball. Seabirds pecked at the mud or stood like statues on long spindly legs.

The oyster bar we were headed for was bigger than the others and located at the end of a wide mud flat. I drove the wagon right out onto the exposed floor of the bay. Neb's big feet made a *squish-slap* noise as he walked. The oysters on Mama's favorite bar are bigger than those we passed close to shore, some bigger than one of Papa's hands.

"Pull up here," said Mama.

She hitched up her ankle-length skirt and climbed down. I climbed down from the wagon too and began to make my way across the mud flats toward the big oysters.

Mama took a raggedy dishtowel from her basket and said, "Come back! Use this towel so you don't cut your hands on the shells." She handed me the rag and her basket, which contained a short iron pry bar for loosening the shellfish.

We walked to the oyster bed together and gathered purple and white shells until the basket was full. Then we sloshed back to the wagon, where Mama sat on the stool and commenced to shucking, using a sharp narrow-bladed knife fashioned from a railroad spike. She worked quickly, popping open each shell with a twist of her wrist and scraping the oyster into the blue pot.

"Can I shuck some?" I asked.

"No." said Mama. "You take Dora's basket and gather up a mess of oysters for her."

I took Miss Dora's bushel basket and waded through the shallow water to a spot where there were clumps of big oysters peeking from between the waves. I squatted and began prying oysters loose and knocking the little shells off of the big ones like Mama had taught me.

The tide was turning and the water shimmered and made ripples around my ankles. It was a beautiful day with just a hint of a breeze and the water was warm as blood, so I thoroughly enjoyed wading from place to place to collect the choicest shellfish.

I stood and scanned my surroundings, looking for the next clump to tackle, when something sparkling on the muddy bottom caught my eye. It wasn't just water dancing on the rippling wavelets. The light on the water was dazzling white and this was yellow.

I squinted, trying to find it again. Yes, there it was. I took a short step and stooped to retrieve the object that had caught my eye.

It was a flat piece of metal with rough edges. It felt very heavy in my hand. Stamped into the metal was a kind of cross and some letters. A hole had been drilled in the metal above the cross.

"Mama!" I cried. "Mama, look what I found!"

"What is it?" asked Mama. "What's all the excitement?"

I ran to her with the coin clutched in my palm. When I reached the wagon, I opened my hand with a flourish.

Mama smiled excitedly when she saw my treasure.

"Lord, Betty, where did that come from?" she asked.

"The oyster bar," I told her.

I handed her the coin and she examined it closely.

"It's an old coin," said Mama. She rubbed it on her apron to make it sparkle. "I've seen these before. My papa had three he had found at different times when he was net fishing. He used to say they likely came off ships that wrecked trying to reach Apalachicola. That's why your daddy's job is so important. He makes sure sailors can find the pass and make their way to safety even at night and when there's a storm."

"Put this in your pocket," said Mama, handing it back. "It's a keepsake. Someday, when you're grown, you will see it and it will remind you of home. Now, get back to hogging."

I skipped back to Miss Dora's basket and got to work. I could feel the weight of the coin in my pocket. As I harvested oysters, I searched the mud around me for another yellow gleam. After I had filled Miss Dora's basket, Mama helped me carry it back to the wagon. Then we gathered and shucked a second basketful for our family before we headed home.

We stopped to give Miss Dora her oysters and have a glass of iced mint tea. She was fretting over where Butch had got to, as it was almost time to eat lunch and he didn't come when she called. She was still yelling for him when we started for home.

We were rolling along under the pines halfway across the island when something stirred in the undergrowth up ahead. The bushes began to shake, making a raspy rattling sound.

"Oh, Lord, it's a rattler," said Mama.

Old Neb froze in his tracks. Neb is afraid of snakes. He and Mama have that in common. He gave an anxious whinny and took a step backwards.

The shaking stopped and I stood up on my seat to get a better look at the path. I didn't see a snake. I gave the reins a shake. Neb took a tentative step and the bushes shook again.

"Somebody's in those bushes," I said.

Mama nodded slowly and squinted at the underbrush.

"Somebody or something," she said nervously.

"Who's up there?" I yelled.

"Walter, that better not be you and Snooky," Mama said.

No answer.

"Let's go," said Mama.

I shook the reins and clucked and Neb looked over his shoulder at me but didn't budge.

"C'mon, Neb," I said. "It ain't a snake."

"Don't say ain't," said Mama.

I shook the reins and Neb took a few timid steps until the bushes shook violently just a few feet in front of the wagon.

Neb gave a sort of shriek and backed away from the commotion.

Mama stood up to see what was in the bushes.

"Butch Proctor, is that you?" she demanded.

The shaking abruptly stopped. There was a loud disturbance as something retreated into the thick salt myrtle and palmetto growing under the pines.

Old Neb refused to take another step until I got down from the wagon and beat the bushes with a stick and held them back for him to see there were no snakes.

"You be careful," Mama told me. "Watch out for snakes."

"All that noise would have chased away any self-respecting snake," I said.

As I pushed the bushes back, I noticed something strange. A clump of wet black seaweed was tangled in the branches of the salt myrtle bush.

When we finally reached home, Evelyn and Cap'n were still on the porch busy with their blocks. Walter and Snooky were nowhere to be seen.

The boys came around the corner of the house as Mama lifted the pot of oysters from the wagon.

"I thought I told you to stay with these children," she scolded.

"We did," said Walter, "I just had to use the necessity."

"We weren't gone but a minute," said Snooky.

Mama eyed them suspiciously.

"Can we go fishing now?" asked Walter.

"You unharness this horse and give him some water. Then wash your hands and come have lunch," said Mama. "Then we'll talk about fishing and about who was playing tricks in the bushes a few minutes ago."

Mama sniffed. Then her face fell.

"My custard!" she blurted. "Where is my custard?" she demanded, looking hard at Snooky and Walter.

The boys stared back blankly.

"Somebody must have took it," said Walter. "It wasn't us."

Snooky looked at his shoes.

"If you were here with Cap'n and your sister, you should have seen who took it," said Mama.

"We might have been in the yard throwing a ball," said Walter, "but we didn't go far."

"Then who took the custard?" demanded Mama.

Both boys shrugged.

"I think my mama's calling me," said Snooky and ran off.

When Papa came to the kitchen for lunch, Mama told him about the "snake" in the brush.

"You worry too much about snakes," he told her.

She told him about the custard and that concerned him more. He had a stern talk with Walter, who insisted he hadn't taken it or seen the culprit. Papa took Walter to the lighthouse for the afternoon to help paint the steps to the light. Of course, they were to be painted green as the Lighthouse Service had allotted Papa ten gallons of green paint two years ago, which he was still trying to use up. When Walter came home for supper, he had specks of paint that looked like green freckles all across his nose.

That night Mama rolled the oysters in seasoned cornmeal and fried them. They were so big that I could only eat two. The taste of them told us summer had begun.

I showed Papa and Walter my treasure then and Papa examined the coin carefully, turning it over and over in his hand. He tested the weight in his palm.

"This is gold," he said thoughtfully. "Where did you find it?"

"Mama's oyster bar," I told him.

"Yent Bar," said Mama.

Papa nodded and handed the coin back to me.

"Do you have someplace safe to put that?" he asked me.

"My sock drawer," I told him.

"Ah," he said. "Go hide it and let it be a family secret."

"Yes, Papa," I told him.

"Let me see," demanded Walter. "Ain't I part of the family?"

"Don't say ain't," said Mama.

I handed Walter the coin. He held it in the palm of his hand and then bit it.

"Don't do that," said Mama.

"I was testing to see if it's really gold," Walter told her.

"And is it?" asked Papa, a smile flickering across his face.

"I don't know," admitted Walter, "but I seen 'em do it in a picture at the Dixie."

"Don't try everything you see in the movies," Papa told him, chuckling.

That night, after examining the coin carefully a dozen times, I wrapped it in a pink hanky and put it carefully away.

Chapter 3

EARLY in June we got a surprise.

A school friend of ours, Neel, had lost his father in a boating accident. This made us all very sad when we heard, but the drowning was just the beginning of the problems for the Henrys. They were left with no income. Mama Sue Henry, as we all called her, had to find a way to feed Neel and his sister. She took in lodgers and earned extra money sewing. Neel, who was only ten, went to work too. He helped at the newspaper office before school and delivered his mother's seamstress work after school. Sometimes he net fished for mullet, which sold for a penny a pound at the seafood houses along Water Street, or gigged flounder, which brought a little more. Their friends in Apalachicola tried to help the Henry family, but it was rough going.

Neel's daddy had given him a special present on his eighth birthday,

Prince, a strapping black pony. Sadly, Mama Sue realized that she could not afford to feed Prince, and it was decided among the parents he would come and live with us.

One bright Saturday morning, a fishing boat arrived at government dock.

Snooky and I were messing about in the *Queen of the Sea*, a little sailboat Papa and Mr. Frank had built for us children to learn to sail. Cap'n and Walter were net fishing without much success. Old Neb stood on the shore nibbling on young palmetto fronds.

It was unusual to have an unexpected visitor, so we all were curious to see what the big boat wanted. *Daphne Mae* was not a boat that regularly visited the island with supplies and she didn't seem to be in any distress. When Snooky and I sailed close to her, we recognized our friend Neel standing by the railing. He waved half-heartedly when he saw us. Behind him was his pony, Prince.

Daphne Mae docked and a man jumped ashore. To our surprise, Papa came walking down the track from the lighthouse as if he expected the arrival. Papa and Mr. Disantis, who owned the *Daphne Mae,* shook hands while we clambered ashore to see what was happening.

When we reached the dock, Papa and the captain were securing a ramp and there on the deck of the boat was Neel holding Prince's beautiful red bridle. The pony sported a matching red saddle with shiny silver trim. We watched in wonder as Neel led Prince onto the dock and then to the shore.

Old Neb was watching too. He snorted unhappily when Neel handed the bridle to Walter.

"He's yours now," said Neel. "Prince can't live with us anymore. I'm too busy working to see to him, so I want you to have him. Will you be good to him?"

"Of course I will," said Walter. "But I can't take him. He's yours."

"I'm too old for Prince now," said Neel. "I've got my family to take care of. He'll be happier here."

"But he's yours," insisted Walter.

Papa put his hand on Walter's shoulder, "Thank Neel, son," he said. "But . . ."

"We will take good care of Prince," Papa told Neel, "and you can come see him whenever you want. You know you are always welcome here."

"Thank you, sir," said Neel.

"Thank you, Neel," said Walter, who was near tears.

Gravely Walter and Neel shook hands.

Miss Dora Proctor was watching from the porch of her house, twisting her blue frilled apron in her hands.

"Will you stay for lunch?" Papa asked.

"No, sir, I need to get on home," said Neel. He reached out to touch Prince's mane and Mr. Disantis put a gentle hand on his shoulder.

Papa shook hands first with Neel and then with Mr. Disantis and they climbed back on the boat and left. Neel never looked back at us and he never came back to visit Prince.

Big tears rolled down Walter's cheeks as he watched the *Daphne Mae* sail away. We were all very quiet. Miss Dora shook her head and went back into her house, closing the door quietly behind her.

"But Papa," said Walter, "Prince belongs to Neel. Neel loves Prince."

Papa knelt to face Walter on his own level.

"Prince belongs to you now. You promised to take care of him. Neel did a very brave thing and he did the right thing. You need to do the same," said Papa. "Now you take that pony home and see to him."

As we led Prince past Old Neb, the big horse opened his eyes wide and whinnied. He sniffed at Prince until Walter told him, "Leave off, Neb," and pushed him away.

Neb trailed along behind us as we led Prince home and stood in the barn door watching intently while we fed and watered the pony.

That afternoon we all fussed over Prince, who seemed to enjoy the attention. Nobody paid much attention to Neb.

The next morning, when I went out to the barn with Walter to check on Prince, we were surprised to see that Neb was standing in a stall that was empty.

"What are you doing here, Neb?" I asked him, tugging at his mane.

His big eyes traveled from my face to Prince and back to me again and he rolled them unhappily.

"You jealous thing," I told him. "You know I still love you."

He lowered his face for me to stroke and I scratched his forehead and kissed him. When I turned to leave, Neb nipped the seat of my overalls and tugged.

"Stop it, Neb!" I told him and he let go.

When we brought hay to Prince and Papa's saddle horses, Comet and Patches, Neb snorted as if demanding hay of his own. This was unusual, as he preferred green grass. I have to say, Neb didn't touch the hay we brought him. An hour later, when we returned to the barn to take Prince for a ride, Neb's stall stood empty once more.

My mother fell in love with Prince, who was a beautiful pony. She ordered a miniature red buckboard from the Montgomery Ward catalog for him to pull. Miss Dora and the Proctor children came to watch the first time we harnessed Prince to our new toy. Neb followed the Proctors and stood on the sidelines staring glumly at the proceedings.

Papa hitched Prince to the little wooden wagon. The black pony looked grand in harness. Walter and Snooky climbed onto the seat and Walter took the reins to launch the pony cart on its maiden voyage. He shook the reins and urged Prince to go. Prince remained motionless.

Papa went to the pony and patted his rump. "Giddy up, Prince," he said, and tugged at his bridle.

Prince snorted.

Mama retrieved a carrot from the garden and stood in front of Prince waving it enticingly.

"C'mon," she said. "C'mon, Prince."

He looked hard at the carrot and at Mama, blinked, and lay down.

We never did get Prince to pull that cart. In the end, Papa unharnessed him. Only then did the pony climb to his feet to be walked to the paddock and released.

When we returned to put the cart away, Neb was standing where Prince had stood in front of the pony cart as if volunteering to pull it. It was a silly idea because he was much too large for the little cart and Mama laughed out loud when she saw him. Papa slapped him on the flank and told him, "Get on now, Neb. You'll break that wagon if you step on it."

The Proctors headed home for supper with Neb following them, his head hanging down and his gait even slower than usual. Walter and I went back to the barn to gaze at Prince until it was time to eat.

A few days later, Papa said we would get a goat to pull the cart. He hooked up Neb to the wagon and all of us children plus Snooky and his sisters piled in along with Papa and Trixie. We drove to Goat Island at the west end of St. George and all climbed out.

Papa told Trixie, "Go cut a goat out of that herd to pull the new wagon." He pointed at the herd.

Amazingly, Trixie seemed to understand. After listening intelligently, she dashed into the center of the flock and separated a beautiful billy goat with black spots and large horns. Papa put a rope on the goat and tied him to the wagon to lead him home. The next morning Papa hooked him up to the red wagon. Billy acted as if he had spent his whole life in harness. Walter and Snooky climbed back on the wagon, Walter shook the reins, and off they went.

For years to come, we would return Billy to his herd on Goat Island at the end of summer and release him. Each spring he would come to us when we called and return to the lighthouse to spend vacation with his adopted family. He loved carrots and crusts of bread, but he'd eat anything green, including the needles on a low pine branch. He and Prince became fast friends and shared a stall when Billy was visiting the lighthouse.

Lois Swoboda

Chapter 4

ALTHOUGH Prince refused to pull a cart, he didn't mind his saddle and we loved to ride him. It was different from riding Neb, who was always bareback and made most of the decisions about where the ride would go, although sometimes you could get him to turn by pulling on his mane. Also, Neb traveled at one speed—slow.

Prince was easy to steer by tugging at his red leather reins. He pranced with his neck arched when he was saddled as if he was proud of his finery. He was docile enough to carry Cap'n and Evelyn but he could be induced to trot or even gallop with a gentle kick in the ribs. Walter, Snooky, and I would speed along the beach, splashing in the surf, and then spend an hour brushing his coat and cleaning his tack.

I am ashamed to say that, lured by the pretty pony, we somewhat neglected Old Neb. Nevertheless, he still followed us about like a big faithful hound and begged for bread and apples when we ate a picnic lunch.

On the island, there's a lot to do. We swim and fish, chase each other across dunes or slide down them in cardboard grocery boxes. We climb like monkeys in the big live oak trees and swing from the branches like Tarzan the Ape Man.

At my mother's kitchen door is a ship's bell that she rings at meal times. The rule is that we are not to go out of earshot of that bell, which can be heard about half a mile away, and we must return home immediately when it rings. We have explored every inch of the island from shore to shore within that span. We made a fort in a "cave" under a little scrub oak tree overgrown with greenbrier. It is so thickly roofed with leaves you can shelter inside from the rain.

Early in June, Snooky, Walter, and I took lamps and other supplies to camp at our fort overnight. Miss Dora and Mama were not entirely happy with the expedition. Mama fretted aloud about snakes, but Papa said it would do us good to learn self-reliance.

We set up camp and built a driftwood fire to cook wieners on sticks and heat a can of beans. Each of us had carried a pillow and a blanket to wrap up in when it was time for bed. Trixie joined us for the evening.

We felt very adventuresome sitting around the fire as the moon rose and the stars winked on. We could hear owls hooting in the trees and waves lapping on the shore. Way out over the water lightning flashed, but where we sat there was barely a hint of wind and the stars twinkled overhead.

"Butch says there's panthers on this island," said Snooky.

"No such thing," said Walter. "I ain't never seen a panther here."

"Butch said you don't see them but they watch you from the trees at night."

We all looked around a little nervously. Walter took a stick from the fire and lit the lantern we had brought along.

"If there's panthers here, why don't we ever see any tracks?" I asked.

"Panthers are real sneaky," said Snooky.

"Well, what do they eat?" Walter wanted to know.

"Butch said they eat rabbits."

"There ain't no rabbits on this island," scoffed Walter.

"That's 'cause the panthers ate them."

"Well, if the rabbits are all gone," said Walter, "what do they eat now?"

This seemed to stump Snooky and we fell silent. The fire had begun to dissolve into embers and it was clear we needed more wood to build it up.

"I'm going for some more wood," said Walter. He stood and picked up the kerosene lamp.

"I'm coming too," said Snooky.

"Me too," I said rising.

"No," said Walter. "You stay here with the camp."

"Why?" I demanded.

"Somebody needs to stay here and watch things," he insisted.

"I'm older than you. You stay," I said.

"Are you scared?" he countered.

"No!" I said.

"Then prove it!" Walter said.

"Fine!" I said. "Trixie, you stay with me!"

I sat back down and began poking the fire with a stick as Walter and

Snooky disappeared into the shadows. Trixie watched them go, looked at me, and whined.

"What?" I asked her.

She whimpered pitifully. She looked from me to the path and back at me again with her forehead wrinkled and her ears standing up.

"Oh, all right, you go too," I told her.

She trotted off happily after Walter and Snooky. I could hear foliage rustling and faint voices as they made their way to the beach and I could see the light from the lantern bobbing among the palmettos.

The camp seemed darker after Trixie left and it didn't help that the fire was rapidly failing. I wrapped myself in my blanket, even though I wasn't cold, and listened intently for Walter and Snooky's return. To keep myself company, I began to sing.

"Rock of ages, cleft for me,

Let me hide myself in thee . . ."

Nearby in the woods, there was a loud thump, as if something heavy had dropped from a tree, and a twig cracked.

"Walter," I called, "is that you?"

No answer.

"Snooky? Y'all come out now. I know it's you and I am not scared so just come on out."

Something moved, rattling the palmettos. I picked up a burning stick out of the fire and stood, letting my blanket drop to the ground.

"Walter!" I yelled. "Stop it, Snooky. You better come out. You're both gonna get in trouble if you don't."

Just outside the circle of firelight, a bush began to shake violently and I screamed.

"Papa! Papa!"

I heard the sound of a door slamming and the pounding of running feet all around me. Papa appeared first and I dropped my stick and ran to him. He held my shoulders and asked, "What's the matter?"

"I heard something in the woods," I sobbed.

"Where's your brother?" asked Papa.

"I don't know," I wailed. "I think the panther may have got him."

"A panther?" asked Papa.

"Snooky said there are panthers on the island."

"No such thing," said Papa. "Where's your brother?" he asked again.

"I'm here, Papa," said Walter. "Snooky and me went to get wood."

"And left your sister alone?" demanded Papa.

"She said she wasn't scared," said Walter.

"Well, I think we've had enough of camping for one night," said Papa. "You gather up your things and come back to the house with me. Your mama was worried sick and now she's scared to death."

"But Papa," said Walter, "me and Snooky ain't scared."

"Don't say ain't and don't talk back," said Papa.

We were herded back to the house, carrying our blankets and pillows, and put to bed. Mama fussed over us and insisted we all have hot milk. She gave Papa a dark look.

Lying in bed, I could still hear Mama and Papa fussing. I was humiliated to have brought the camping adventure to a bad end.

When I woke up the next morning, Old Neb was staring at me through my bedroom window. I climbed out of bed and ran outside to see him and he met me at the front door.

"What are you doing here?" I asked.

All he could do was snuffle, but it was a friendly noise. I scratched his nose and kissed him.

After breakfast, Papa carried Snooky home on Comet and Mama made it clear there would be no more campouts. Walter was furious.

"You dang girls ruin everything," he said. "You are just a bunch of dang babies."

"There really was something in the woods," I told him.

He gave a disgusted grunt.

I was ashamed to have acted such a coward and determined to prove myself at the first opportunity.

Snooky's Mama kept him home the rest of the day. That afternoon, Walter and I were sent back to our campsite to fetch a skillet we had left behind. Walter refused to speak to me on the way.

"Don't be mad. I did hear something in the woods," I told him.

When we reached the fire circle, I went straight to the bush that had given me such a fright the night before.

"Look here," I tried to show Walter. "There's fresh broken branches."

"Leave that alone and help me find the skillet," he said.

But the skillet was nowhere to be found.

We had to return home and give that bad news to Mama, who was not pleased. When Papa came home around suppertime, she told him about the missing pan.

"It's my little one," she said. "The one I like to use to make milk gravy."

"Well, it must be there," he said. "Skillets don't grow legs and walk. Betty and I will go and find it."

After supper, he said, "Come on, Betty," and took my hand.

"Watch out for snakes," said Mama.

"Don't worry," said Papa.

"Take your bonnet, Betty," said Mama, chasing me onto the porch with the pink abomination clutched in her fist.

"It's almost dark," I argued.

"Take it!" said Mama.

"Put it on," Papa said seriously.

Mama tied it under my chin.

Together Papa and I set off. Once we had crossed the dunes Papa asked, "You don't much like your bonnet, do you?"

"It has pink ruffles," I complained.

"If you promise me you'll wear that bonnet for now, I'll talk to Mama about finding you another hat."

"Oh, thank you, Papa," I told him.

"What frightened you so last night?" asked Papa.

"I think I heard a panther. I'm sorry. I didn't mean to scare everybody."

"Everybody gets scared sometimes," said Papa. "It's nothing to be sorry for."

"You don't get scared," I said.

"Oh, I've been scared," he said smiling down at me, "and not just when I was a little boy."

"Were you scared last night?" I asked him.

"I was worried," he answered. "Your Mama was scared and she's still a little bit upset. She worries about you children more than you know."

"She worries about snakes," I said. "I know that."

"Not just snakes," he said. "She loves you very much so she worries about anything she thinks might hurt you. I want you to understand that."

By now, we had reached the camp and Papa and I began to look around for the skillet.

I checked inside the fort but the skillet wasn't there. When I poked my head out, Papa asked, "What exactly did you hear last night?"

"I was sitting here by the fire," I said walking to the spot. "Walter and Snooky had gone to the beach. I was by myself and it was dark and, all of a sudden, there was a big thump, just like a panther jumping down out of a tree."

"Had you been talking about panthers?" asked Papa.

I nodded. Just remembering the noises in the dark made my shoulders twitch and my mouth feel cottony.

"Why did the subject come up?" asked Papa as he poked around in the bushes.

"Snooky said Butch told him there was panthers on the island."

"Butch said that?" asked Papa.

I nodded.

"But none of you has ever seen a panther?"

I shook my head.

"And I have never seen a panther," said Papa.

I nodded.

"But I heard something, I really did," I told him. "I heard something big jump down out of a tree and Snooky had just told us that panthers watch from the trees at night and I just thought . . ."

"Where did the sound come from?" asked Papa.

I pointed and he pushed through the bushes to a tree in the right general direction and began searching the ground around the trunk.

"We never had the pan over there, Papa," I said.

"I guess not," said Papa.

He reached down and picked up something off the ground. Then he held his hand close in front of his face to examine his find.

"What is it, Papa?" I asked.

"Just a thread," said Papa. "A blue thread from a pair of dungarees. I know what you thought and I understand why," he continued. "The important thing is that you understand that there are no panthers on the island and nothing to be afraid of."

"Yes, Papa."

"Now I guess it's time we head for home."

"What about the skillet?"

"I guess I was wrong," said Papa. "It looks like it did grow legs and walk away. You let me worry about that."

He dropped the thread on the sand and took my hand again.

Chapter 5

FOR a few days, Walter and Snooky refused to include me in their games.

During that time they would sneak off together, leaving me alone. Papa would have made them take me if I asked, but somehow I knew that was a bad idea. I kept company with Neb or moped around the kitchen with Mama until she either shooed me away or put me to work.

I spent one morning in the parlor standing Papa's dominoes on end in patterns and knocking them down so that they fell one after the other. I was building a castle out of cards when Cap'n chased Evelyn into the room and knocked it down. I shrieked and began to chase the two of them, which caught Mama's attention at once and she stormed in and stared at the three of us. Evelyn was in tears and Cap'n was red-faced with his hands balled into fists.

"What are you doing to Cap'n and your sister?" she demanded.

"I wasn't doing anything . . ." I began.

She surveyed the room with the fallen dominoes still lying in their elaborate curlicues and circles and playing cards everywhere.

"Betty, you are the oldest," she said and I cringed. It was never a good sign when people reminded me I was the oldest. "I expect more of you. If you can't help around the house, you must try, at least, to not make a mess. This is the parlor where we welcome guests and just look at it."

"But nobody's going to come and visit today," I argued. "It isn't Sunday. Nobody but Miss Dora ever comes to visit except on Sunday and she sits in the kitchen with you."

"Don't sass me!" said Mama, ignoring my very reasonable observation. After all, we lived on an island. People didn't just drop in.

"But . . ." I began.

"You clean up this mess, Betty, and when you finish, if you can't find something to do outside, go to your room."

"Yes'm," I muttered.

I set to work picking up the dominoes and putting them in their wooden box, which I returned to its place atop the piano.

Then I gathered up the cards. There were two decks but I just squared off the edges and put them back in their little cardboard boxes without sorting them. Since they all had red backs, I hoped nobody would notice. Then I went into my room and rummaged through my sock drawer to find my coin so I could look at it. I found the pink hanky but the coin was gone. I pulled socks out and threw them on the floor but my treasure had vanished.

I shoved that drawer closed and pulled out the one below it, which contained underwear and T-shirts.

I was frantically tossing them into a heap at my feet when Mama walked past my open door. I heard her stop and I froze. She returned to the doorway to stare at me in disbelief.

"What are you doing?" she gasped.

"I can't find my coin!"

"But what are you doing? Look at your room," she said, her voice trembling with anger.

"But I can't find my coin. It's gone."

"Look at your room," she insisted.

I looked around and I had to admit it was a mess. Clothes were strewn everywhere.

"I can clean it up," I said sheepishly, "but first I have to find my coin. It's gone."

"Betty, I am very disappointed in you. First, you make a mess of the parlor and now this. What do you have to say for yourself?"

"I can clean it up," I said again, looking around me.

"You will clean it up right now," said Mama. "Perhaps if you took better care of your things, you wouldn't have lost your coin. I imagine it will turn up. Now get to work and have everything put away before your father comes home for supper!"

"But I didn't lose it. It was here . . ."

Mama cut me off. "No back talk, miss. You get this cleaned up before Papa comes home and then come help me in the kitchen."

"Yes, ma'am," I said, pushing at a pair of yellow socks with one bare toe.

At supper I had to listen to Mama complain to Papa about my behavior. He took her side and told me to act my age. Walter had supper at Snooky's house and later in the afternoon he came home with a big string of mullet he had caught net fishing and everybody acted like he was some kind of hero. Mama fixed fried green tomatoes for dinner because they were his favorite. Even Papa wasn't interested in hearing about my missing coin.

A few days later at breakfast, Papa told Mama he had a taste for some of her oyster stew.

"I'll cook some up for dinner," she told him, and soon after he and Trixie left for work.

Mama and I loaded the wagon with her stool and tools and Cap'n and Evelyn and we set off for the oyster bar.

Walter and Snooky had left to go fishing before breakfast, taking cold biscuits, cheese, and smoked mullet for a picnic.

Once again, Mama stopped to talk to Miss Dora and offer to bring her oysters and, once again, she said, "Yes, please."

I was sent to fetch a basket from the shed since Butch was nowhere around. When I came back, Mama and Miss Dora were sitting in the kitchen sipping hot coffee. Dooley, Honey, Cap'n, and Evelyn were all drinking lemonade from little green glass teacups.

Old Neb was grazing contentedly on a patch of grass and a few of Miss Dora's daylilies when Mama decided it was time to go.

We set off, leaving the little ones with Miss Dora and, as always, Neb made his unhurried way to Mama's oyster bar without being told.

We were not prepared for what greeted us there. Although the tide had tried to repair the damage, great holes had been gouged in the mud and the clusters of big oysters lay shattered and partly buried in the mud and sand.

Mama gasped.

The bar was effectively ruined. No oysters would be harvested here for the rest of the summer.

"Who would do such a thing?" she wondered aloud.

"What should we do, Mama?" I asked.

Mama just shook her head. Even Old Neb seemed stunned at the sight.

Mama said, "Well, we'll just have to look for another place. Let's go farther down the beach. I've collected oysters on the peninsula at Pilot Cove."

I clucked my tongue and shook the reins.

Neb looked questioningly over his shoulder and I nodded to the west. "Giddy up, Neb," I told him. "It's okay."

He shuffled on along the beach.

"What do you think happened?" I asked Mama.

"I don't know," she said in an unsteady voice. "It looks like somebody did that on purpose. But I can't think why. It's such a shame. I just can't imagine anybody . . ." Mama's voice trailed off and she had a look on her face as if she could imagine who would do such a thing.

We didn't talk much during the rest of the expedition. We had to make three stops to get the oysters we needed, as there weren't many places with big oysters close enough to shore to hog, especially during the summer when the tides were higher.

When we returned to the Proctor house, Mama left me to watch the children and went with Miss Dora into another room to talk. When they returned, Miss Dora looked even paler than usual.

At home, over a supper of leftover fried chicken and greens, Mama told Papa what had happened and he looked very serious.

"Betty, did you tell me you lost your coin?" he asked me.

"I didn't lose it," I told him. "It's just gone."

He frowned.

That night, Papa came home from the lighthouse early and when Snooky and Walter came trailing in, he took them out to the barn. They were gone for quite a while.

Mama was finishing up the stew, adding fresh milk and tasting it for salt and pepper, but every so often, I caught her looking out the kitchen door with a worried expression.

When Papa and Walter returned Snooky was not with them.

"Joseph has gone home," said Papa, "and Walter is going to his room to think."

"Without dinner?" asked Mama.

"Without dinner," Papa confirmed, sending my brother away with a gesture.

After Walter left, Papa said, "You can take him something later, Rachel."

We all sat down at the table and though the stew was good and served with bread still warm from the oven, I didn't feel hungry. I couldn't understand what was going on and that made me very nervous.

For the next few days, Walter went to work with Papa. Even after he was allowed to remain at the house, he wasn't allowed to leave and Snooky was shy about visiting for a week.

When Snooky finally did show up, the remains of a shiner encircled his left eye with an aura of purple and green.

"What happened to your eye?" asked Mama, bending to examine it.

"It's okay. I fell down," said Snooky, turning away.

Walter looked shocked. He grabbed Snooky's shoulders and stared hard at his face.

"C'mon," Walter said abruptly, and they bolted toward the barn. I wanted to follow but Mama made me fetch my bonnet and, by the time I got it from my room Snooky and Walter had vanished.

I went into the barn and, not finding the boys, climbed into the hayloft. I was feeling lonely and a little sorry for myself. I was drifting off to sleep amid the warm smell of livestock and the dappled light filtering through the walls when Snooky and Walter entered. They didn't know I was there.

I was about to call to them when Walter said, "Why did he hit you?"

"Same as always," said Snooky. "For meanness."

"Did you ask him for it back?" asked Walter.

Snooky shook his head and kicked at the rough floorboards.

"Did you tell your mom?" asked Walter.

"Of course not. I ain't a snitch," said Snooky.

"Ain't you scared of him?" asked Walter.

"I'm scared what he'd do if I tell," said Snooky.

"Did Butch black your eye, Snooky?" I blurted out.

The two boys jumped and stared up at me open-mouthed. Walter ran to the wooden hayloft ladder and scrambled up with Snooky hard on his heels. We wrestled and I fell back on the hay with Walter straddling me, his hand held over my mouth.

"You can't tell!" he said.

I shoved him off and stood up.

"Oh, yes, I can," I snarled.

"You'll be a snitch," said Walter, "and Butch will kill us all."

"Papa won't let him," I said.

"You'll be a snitch!" said Walter.

"If he's beating Snooky up, you have to tell," I argued.

"Snitch!" said Snooky.

Walter grabbed my arm and twisted it behind my back.

"Ouch! Let go of me!" I said and tried to break away.

"Promise you won't tell," demanded Walter.

"I promise," I mumbled. He let go of my arm.

Just then Papa entered the barn and looked up at us.

"What's all the fuss?" he asked.

Snooky and Walter looked at me with questioning eyes.

"Nothing," I said. "We were just playing."

"Well, come on down," said Papa. "Your mama needs some help with the weeding."

Things returned to normal for a while, although Walter and Snooky stayed close to the house. They were never out of sight these days. They treated me better now that we shared the secret about Butch.

We swam in the hot afternoons. Sometimes Mama came along. Dolphins played along the shore and raced after fish. We tried to swim out to meet them, but we never could.

Mama relented somewhat about the bonnet and allowed me to wear one of her old straw hats. It had some blue silk flowers, but they fell off.

For chores, we helped in the garden with the weeding and picking. We fed the chickens and the other livestock and swept the porch with a stick broom Papa made.

Thunderstorms formed in the late afternoon. We would sit on the deep sheltering porches and watch the surf, the pouring rain, and the lightning shattering the sky. Sometimes a waterspout would drop from the black ceiling of clouds and dance across the water, curling and twisting like a snake. Once we saw a pair materialize like twins and march along the beach together just offshore.

When the subject of campouts was raised, Mama wouldn't even discuss another overnight adventure. Papa came to our rescue.

He returned from a trip to town for supplies with an army surplus tent and several cots. He erected the tent by the dunes, where it could clearly be seen from the house. We used it as a fort at first. Eventually Walter, Snooky, and I were allowed to camp overnight occasionally, taking Trixie along for protection.

On summer nights, we chased crabs and lay on the beach watching for shooting stars. Papa taught us the constellations and planets. The waves shimmered with light from billions of tiny glowing animals and the sea spray looked like white sparks. During full moons, the horseshoe crabs crawled ashore to mate. We watched the huge sea turtles creep up out of the water too, to dig their nests and deposit their eggs, shedding a tear for each one laid. Later, the baby turtles dug their way free from the sand and raced for the water, hundreds at a time.

I am not frightened of much of anything on the island but Mama worries. We see a snake from time to time but they are always more afraid of you than you are of them. Papa won't kill them. He picks them up and carries them over the dunes while Mama hides in the kitchen. She worries about gators too. They live in the freshwater ponds, hanging in the water half covered by algae and weeds, with their lizard eyes watching everything. We keep a respectful distance and keep Trixie close by us as Papa says gators have a natural taste for dogs.

The ocean is dangerous, I guess, although we all swim like fish. Sharks don't scare me much. I never knew anyone to get bit, though Mama says it happens all the time. I do worry about stingrays and learned from an early age to shuffle my feet in the surf to avoid stepping on one.

At the end of June, Walter forgot to shuffle and went running into the surf one early morning. He got stung by a ray. He yelped and then cried like a baby while I ran home for help. He had to sit with his foot propped up and wrapped in an old towel. Papa carried him to the porch every morning and to bed every night for weeks and weeks. I brought him shells and Indian pottery I found on the beach and we made a collection.

Snooky faithfully sat with Walter on many afternoons, playing checkers and dominoes and eating Mama's oatmeal cookies and fig preserves. Sometimes Snooky joined me beachcombing, but more often it was Neb who followed along and joined me in the surf when I took a dip to cool off. I would scramble onto his back and hug his neck as he waded into the ocean. Sometimes I shared an apple or cookies with him for a snack and I let him think I was surprised when he shambled up behind me and blew against the back of my neck with his big warm lips.

One day, when I was scouring the beach for potsherds, I found a chain about eight inches long with wide half-inch links. It was heavy and covered in algae but not rusted. I took it along to Walter and we put it in the sun to dry. When the algae flaked away, we could see that there was a pattern worked into the black metal. We tucked it in a cigar box with our pottery and promptly forgot it.

The Pierces, who own St. Vincent Island and visit there in the winter, are well off. When they heard about Walter's stung foot, they sent old copies of *John Martin's Book,* a magazine for children, for him to look at. There were three whole years of issues except for November 1929.

These became a family treasure as there was no library and books were scarce. Snooky, Walter, and I read and reread them, although Butch said they were babyish. They were full of stories about cowboys, kings, fairies, and pirates. There were also riddles and jingles to learn by heart. Walter, who was never one for school, being more a man of action, learned to read pretty well while he was laid up, so, in a way, he was lucky to get stung.

Snooky's daddy, Mr. Frank, works in Apalachicola as a bookkeeper and over most of the summer he only visits on weekends. He is a smart man and knows a lot about the history of the islands. He has a big collection of pottery, blown glass bottles, and other flotsam he keeps on shelves at the bay house.

On Sundays, Miss Dora always cooks up a big dinner and carries it to our house where the families enjoy it together. We children play on the beach all day while the adults exchange news and listen to the Victrola or play cards and dominoes. In the evening, Miss Dora plays the guitar and sometimes we sing along, especially Papa, who has a beautiful voice.

Late on Sunday nights, Mr. Frank hitches Neb up to the buckboard and loads up the dishes, as well as Honey and Dooley, who are most often asleep. Neb takes the Proctor family home. Papa sends me and Walter to collect the wagon in the morning.

One Sunday, Mr. Frank asked to see our pottery collection. Walter produced our treasures housed in three cigar boxes and Mr. Frank admired them with polite enthusiasm until he saw the length of chain. He examined it carefully and seemed to be very excited by what he saw. He asked Mama for baking soda, a bowl, and boiling water. She brought these. Mr. Frank unwrapped a piece of tin foil off a stick of gum he popped into his mouth. He placed the foil in the bottom of the bowl and coiled the chain on top of it. Then he poured out enough soda to cover the chain and poured boiling water from a kettle over the whole arrangement. As we all watched, the soda bubbled up white and the chain's black color melted away to reveal a shining silver surface buried beneath the tarnish.

Mr. Frank like to have burned his fingers fetching that chain out of the water. Grinning broadly, he held it glittering in the sun. The chain was solid silver engraved with a pattern of tiny flowers. It was passed from hand to hand and admired. Even Butch seemed interested.

Mr. Frank asked where I had found it and I said I would show him. I felt very important when everyone traipsed after me. Even Old Neb joined the parade with Walter on his back. I led them to a stretch of beach where the wooden hull of a wrecked shrimp boat was partly buried in the sand. Mr. Frank carried a shovel he had fetched from the barn. I was sure of the spot, as I had found the chain right next to the bow of the old boat. Everyone began to kick at the sand as if hoping to find the rest of the chain and Mr. Frank dug a trench right around that bow but nothing else appeared.

Mama and Miss Dora were the first to tire of the search and, taking the little girls, they headed back to the kitchen to lay out the evening meal. Butch soon bored of the treasure hunt as well. Papa said he had to do a few chores before supper.

Mr. Frank, me, Snooky, Cap'n, and Walter—still seated on Neb—continued to search the beach until the dinner bell sounded. Then we headed back to the lighthouse.

Over dinner, the conversation turned to the chain and its origin. Mama said she imagined it must have come off the wrecked shrimp boat but Miss Dora said she doubted that because it was too fine. She thought it must have belonged to a lady. Papa said we would never know how the chain got to our island and it didn't matter as many strange things washed up on the shore. Mama asked Mr. Frank where he thought the chain had come from. He swallowed a mouthful of mashed potatoes and gravy and smiled.

"I can't be sure," he said, "but there were privateers here in the old days and that chain could have come off a treasure ship."

"What's privateers?" I asked.

Butch chuckled in a mean kind of way like I had said something very stupid. Mr. Frank gave him a hard look.

"Pirates," explained Mr. Frank kindly. "Privateers is another word for pirates."

"Were there really pirates here?" demanded Walter.

Mr. Frank said, "Yes, indeed, there were pirates here and one in particular. The notorious villain William Augustus Bowles was headquartered on this island for a time. He had not one but two pirate ships with crews of renegade Indians and runaway slaves. He raided many a Spanish treasure ship in his time, and some say he buried treasure all along the coast."

Walter's eyes were as big as sand dollars and Snooky stopped chewing his food. We had read about pirates and all their habits in *John Martin's Book*. The chain seemed proof positive that there was probably treasure hidden all over the island.

I thought back to the coin I had found.

Butch was very quiet and still as his father spoke. I think he was listening very hard.

"I found a gold coin," I said.

Mr. Frank raised his eyebrows.

"I heard about that," said Mr. Frank. "Somebody said it got lost."

"It disappeared," I told him. "One day it was in my sock drawer and the next day it was gone."

"Is that so?" asked Mr. Frank, and he looked at Butch.

Butch looked at his plate.

After that day, I carried a little folding trench shovel with me on all my walks. Cap'n, Snooky, and I returned to the shrimp boat and excavated thoroughly for fifteen feet around it, disturbing quite a number of crabs in the process. Cap'n chased them but luckily never caught one. Neb stood on the dunes watching us as he munched sea oats.

We found nothing, but were not discouraged. Snooky and I widened our search, first digging trenches along the beach and then carrying our explorations inland. We found no treasure but did unearth more pottery, including a pottery alligator head and a little Indian pottery bowl with a design of dots and curling lines that was perfect and unchipped. We also found a few buttons, rusty bolts, bottles both whole and broken, musket balls, and half a dozen arrowheads.

Sometimes I had the strangest feeling that we were not alone, but Snooky didn't seem to notice. I never saw anyone. It was just a feeling. Old Neb nearly always followed us on these expeditions and he seemed to stand watch.

One afternoon, digging out behind the chicken coop in a likely stretch of sand, we found Mama's missing skillet.

"Don't that beat all?" said Snooky.

That day, Cap'n had joined us since we were close to home.

"How'd it get here, Betty?" he asked.

I said I didn't know but I sure was glad we had found it. Mama gave us each a blueberry muffin when we brought it home. Walter, Snooky, and I discussed the find at length but we couldn't explain the skillet's mysterious behavior.

Each afternoon, Snooky and I would come home and discuss our findings, or lack thereof, with Walter. When he began to get around a bit with the help of a stick, he was the one who decided we should begin taking Billy and the wagon along with us on our daily forays. This served two purposes—it would provide a means of bringing the treasure home once we found it, and it allowed Walter to come along, as he could ride quite comfortably in the wagon.

Early one morning, Walter, Snooky, and I were treasure hunting when we found a corked bottle with a rolled-up sheet of paper inside half buried in the sand. It stood in the middle of the broad sand beach as if it had washed ashore. Snooky spotted it first. He raced to pick it up and held it high above his head with a whoop.

"What is it?" Walter and I demanded.

"It's a message in a bottle like in the shipwreck story by Mr. Robert Louis Stevenson," said Snooky. "It could be from anywhere, maybe from a stranded sailor in the Sargasso Sea."

I didn't think the bottle looked all that old. In fact, it looked like a ketchup bottle to me, but I didn't say so. Anyway, I supposed there might be ketchup on a stranded ship.

Walter climbed from the goat cart and hobbled to us, leaning on his stick.

We pried the cork from the mouth of the bottle and tried to shake the paper out, but in the end we broke the glass on an old brick to get to the note. It turned out to be a map. The edges of the thick, dirty paper were burned and the map was drawn in red ink . . . or blood.

The map showed a peninsula with some details sketched in. Next to it was a little island with animals standing on it. They were stick goats with curvy horns and thin beards. Another little island had birds.

Waves were sketched around the land to show it was surrounded by water and in a corner of the paper was a skull and crossbones.

At the end of the peninsula was a drawing of a tombstone and nearby five palm trees in a circle, one of which was almost twice the height of the others. In the middle of the circle was an X.

We stared at the map with pounding hearts and Walter's hands shook with excitement.

"This is a treasure map," he said with conviction.

"Is it real?" I asked, wondering how a treasure map got into a ketchup bottle.

"Has to be!" Walter said. "It floated ashore."

"I wonder where it come from," whispered Snooky.

"It could have come from anywhere," said Walter in a hushed voice.

"Well, I know what that's a map of," I said.

Snooky and Walter stared at me.

"Do not!" said Walter.

"Yes, I do," I insisted. "It's here. That's a map of the end of the island.

There's Goat Island where Billy came from and Bird Island," I said pointing. "And that is Lewis Leland's grave, the one on Sand Island. If there's a treasure, it's buried here in this circle of trees."

"I didn't never see a circle of trees over there," said Walter.

"You never looked," I said. "I bet if we went and looked, we'd find those trees."

"What do we do?" asked Snooky, looking to Walter for guidance.

"We go and find it!" said Walter."

"Just us?" asked Snooky.

"You're pure crazy!" I said. "We can't go get it. How would we even get down there?"

"Let me think," said Walter. "Meantime, we don't tell nobody else about this."

He picked up a sliver of the broken ketchup bottle and pricked his finger, then handed the glass to me.

"I'm not doing that," I said.

"Then you're just a big chicken because you're a girl," said Walter.

"It's not because I'm a girl. I just don't want to! "

"Give it to Snooky," said Walter.

Snooky slowly extended his hand and took the glass. Squeezing his eyes shut, he pricked a finger too. His eyes popped open.

"It didn't hurt," declared Snooky, examining the drop of blood oozing from his finger.

"Give it here," I said. I pricked my own finger. It hurt like fire but I wasn't going to say so.

We touched our fingers together to exchange blood and swore to keep our secret.

"What are we going to do with it?" whispered Snooky.

"I'll take it," said Walter and he rolled it back up and shoved it inside his shirt.

He climbed back in the cart.

Up on the dunes, Neb gave a loud whinny. He seemed to be staring at the crest of the dunes further west.

"What is it, Neb?" I asked. "I think he's trying to show us something,"

I told Snooky and Walter and started to climb up to where Neb stood.

"He's a fool horse," said Walter. "What could he want to show us?"

Neb whinnied again and shook his head, and then he took off across the dunes at a fast walk, which was as good as a gallop for Neb.

"What's the matter, Neb?" I yelled.

"Forget him," said Walter. "I want to get this home and hidden."

Now Neb was standing with his back to us staring down the back of the dunes and into the jungle at the center of the island.

When we started back toward the lighthouse discussing the discovery in hushed tones, Neb left off his looking and came plodding after us in his usual way.

After we put Billy up, we found Butch leaning against the barn outside almost as if he was waiting.

"Where have you been?" he demanded with a knowing look in his beady blue eyes.

"Nowhere," said Walter, attempting to limp past the big boy.

"What's the big hurry?" asked Butch, grabbing at Walter's collar from behind.

"Leave him alone, Butch," said Snooky.

Butch looked balefully at his brother.

"You best get home," Butch said, making a fist and pressing it to Snooky's cheek. "Mama wants you for chores."

Snooky cringed. He said "G'bye," and scampered off in the direction of the bay.

Butch turned his attention back to Walter, who was easing closer to the house. Though Butch was much bigger, Walter turned and stood his ground when confronted.

"You got something down the front of your shirt, little girl?" Butch asked Walter, grabbing the strap of his overalls.

"Nope," Walter lied and squared his shoulders trying to look taller.

Butch was closing in on Walter. I had to help my brother, so I grabbed the tail of Butch's shirt and tugged hard.

Neb, who had followed us into the barn, appeared at the door and stared hard at Butch. He pawed the ground and took a step in Butch's direction. Butch suddenly looked a little frightened. He let go of Walter and backed away as the big horse pawed the ground and then took another step toward Butch. It was the first time I had ever seen Neb look mad.

Just then Papa appeared, headed to the barn, and looked at us curiously.

"What's going on here?" he asked.

"Nothing, Papa," said Walter. "We was just playing."

"We *were* just playing," corrected Papa. "You get back to the house and get off that foot. Your mama will skin me if you make it worse."

"Butch, you come along with me," Papa said. "I was about to fetch water for the horses and I'll give you a nickel to help me."

"Yes, sir," said Butch as if butter wouldn't melt in his mealy mouth.

Butch walked off with Papa.

When we went inside to the bedroom Walter shared with Cap'n, Walter unscrewed the top of the bedpost and slid the rolled map into the hollow brass tube, then replaced the cap.

"It will be safe in there until we can work out what to do," he said.

Old Neb appeared outside the window.

"Thanks, Neb," said Walter.

"It's almost like he chased Butch on purpose," Walter told me.

I thought it was more than almost.

Chapter 6

AUGUST had arrived and we had only a month left on St. George. Over the next week, Snooky, Walter, and I discussed ways of getting to the west end of the island.

It was a five-mile walk and, if we found the treasure, we had to have a way to get it home. We decided the answer was Billy and the cart. Walter and Snooky would ride in the goat cart and I would ride Prince. We figured if we left early in the morning, we could reach our destination, find the circle of trees, dig up the treasure, and be home in time for supper. If we didn't find the treasure, nobody had to know we had made the trip. If we did find it and returned home rich, our parents would have to forgive us.

Our effort to retrieve the pirate gold was delayed by a week of stormy weather. It began raining on Friday night and the next five days were punctuated with cloudbursts, thunder, and lightning. We were confined to the house, as Mama is as afraid of lightning as she is of snakes. We spent the days reading and drawing or playing games. Walter and I played hangman and tic-tac-toe. There was a checkerboard and dominoes and a deck of cards for "Go Fish." We joined the little ones in games of hide-and-seek and tag until Mama, driven to distraction by our pent-up energy, put a stop to it. During a period when the rain abated some, she shooed us onto the porch so she could clean the floors. I was put in charge of Evelyn and Cap'n. The thunder had stopped, so we moved our game to the barn. We climbed in the hayloft, petted the saddle horses, and rubbed the milk cow's velvety nose. We hadn't seen Neb all week. He was not a big fan of storms and was probably holed up in his bayside barn.

Me and Walter climbed into the stall with Billy and Prince and hand-fed them hay while Cap'n and Evelyn watched. We opened the stall, led Prince out, and put Evelyn on his back to be guided around the barn. Then Cap'n had a turn. The rain began again, tapping on the tin roof of the barn, and suddenly there was an enormous roar of thunder and lightning blazed through the cracks in the barn walls. The whole building shook, which must have spooked poor Billy. The goat, who had been placidly standing in his stall chewing his cud and watching the proceedings, suddenly bolted. Billy ran from his stall and began racing around the barn. This was an unprecedented event. I ran after him with Walter hopping along behind me, favoring his good foot. We tried to corner Billy but he eluded us and made a mad dash for the door. All four of us children ran to the door to watch as he raced across the yard and up onto the front porch.

Mama, who was also spooked by the lightning, had come to the kitchen door to see what had become of us kids. She reached that door about the same time Billy did but he was not deterred by her presence and pushed right past her and into the kitchen. Mama pursued the frightened goat. The four of us hurried across the yard through the pouring rain, Walter seeming to forget his foot in the excitement, and into the kitchen in time to see Mama and Billy in a standoff.

I ran onto the porch and began to ring the dinner bell to summon Papa. He was working in the lighthouse. He and Trixie had retreated from the crowded house early that morning. When he appeared at the kitchen door, Mama was attempting to remove Billy from the kitchen by brute force using her mop as a weapon. Billy had retreated under the kitchen table and was bleating plaintively.

Papa looked at the goat, the kitchen, us children dripping wet, and Mama brandishing the mop and he began to laugh. Mama seemed about to turn the mop on Papa when she suddenly dissolved into laughter too. Then we were all laughing.

Papa led Billy back to the barn and restored him and Prince to their stall.

We all dried off and put on fresh clothes. Mama put the wet ones in a tub on the porch. Then Walter helped Mama wash and dry the kitchen floor and I amused Evelyn and Cap'n with dominoes until suppertime.

On Thursday afternoon, the weather finally broke and the black clouds trailed away to the north to be replaced by fluffy white ones high up in a beautiful blue sky.

Walter and I took off toward Snooky's house and he met us halfway along the path. We hadn't seen him since Saturday. We climbed an oak tree beside the path. It was still dripping from the week of rain but the air was

Lois Swoboda

very warm out and we didn't care. Seated on a branch up in the crown, we discussed our plans. We decided we would go treasure hunting the next day.

Below us on the trail, a twig cracked. We all fell silent and, in a minute, somebody began to whistle an off-key tune. Butch strode under our hiding place with a fishing net slung over his shoulder on his way to the beach. He didn't seem to notice us at all. After he disappeared along the trail, who should appear on the path below but Old Neb. It seemed as if he was following Butch but he immediately spotted us in the tree and stood staring up expectantly until we climbed town. We took turns riding him down to the bay to launch the *Queen of the Sea* and played there until lunchtime.

That evening at supper, I told Mama that Walter, Snooky, and I wanted to go berry picking the next day. I think Mama was secretly thrilled at the prospect of having us out of the house. She agreed immediately and said we could take a picnic lunch. I asked if we could take the goat cart and Mama and Papa agreed to that too. Everything was going well until Mama observed that Cap'n would enjoy the trip and ought to go along. Walter and I tried to argue against this, but we were overruled.

The next morning, Snooky was knocking on the kitchen door while Walter and I were still eating breakfast. By nine o'clock, we had harnessed Billy and saddled Prince and were headed west along the beach with Walter and Cap'n in the little red goat cart, me on Prince and Snooky walking alongside. Mama waved good-bye from the kitchen door and reminded us to avoid snakes at all costs and not to go into the water for half an hour after lunch.

We had not gone far when Old Neb appeared at the crest of the dunes about fifty feet behind us. He made his way to the beach and caught up with us in short order, apparently having decided to join the safari. This pleased us, as it meant Snooky could ride too. I let him take Prince. I mounted Neb and we set off again. By midmorning, we were halfway to our destination and well beyond our legal boundary when we heard hoofbeats thumping along the beach from the direction of home. Papa, mounted on Comet, was cantering toward us with a stern expression on his suntanned face. We stood transfixed as he pulled the horse to a halt and frowned at us.

"Do you know how far you are from home?" he demanded.

We all said no.

"Nearly three miles!" boomed Papa. "I went to look for Old Neb to haul the wood from a tree that came down in the storm and couldn't find him. I climbed the tower to look for him and saw you. What are you doing way over here?"

"We were just looking for a berry patch, Papa," I said innocently. "We stayed right on the beach."

"Since when do berries grow on the beach?" Papa demanded. "Turn around and follow me home this minute!"

"Yes, sir," we all intoned.

We headed back home in silence. Papa rode beside me and said, "I'm surprised at you, Betty. You are the oldest and I expect you to think more about things. What were you doing so far from home? And don't talk to me about berry picking. Better not to talk at all than lie."

"But Papa . . ."

"I mean it," he said. "Is this some fool thing to do with all this nonsense about treasure? I see you brought along a shovel."

"We didn't know we had got so far," I began.

Papa cut me off with a look.

Mama and Evelyn were coming home from picking beans in the garden when our procession arrived at the lighthouse. Mama watched us make our way to the barn. She shooed Evelyn up to the porch and followed us, her apron still full of beans for supper.

"I don't see any berries," said Mama curiously. "What's all this about?"

"I'll explain later," said Papa sternly. "I have to get back to work now. Snooky is going home and Walter and Betty can go to their rooms for the rest of the day. They are being punished."

"What happened?" asked Mama.

Papa told her where he had found us and she was horrified.

"You took Cap'n all the way down there?" she asked me. "What if there had been a snake? What if a storm had come up?"

"We didn't really know how far it was," I whispered.

Walter, who had so far escaped the worst retribution, remained silent with downcast eyes.

"How could you not know?" demanded Mama. She dumped the beans from her apron into our empty berry basket and knelt before Cap'n.

"Are you all right, little Cap'n," she asked and gave him a hug.

The little traitor reached out and hugged her neck, happy to be the only one of us who wasn't in trouble.

Mama turned to Snooky.

"What do you know about all of this?" she demanded.

"We was just looking for berries," he said. "We didn't know how far we had got."

Mama gave him a chilling look.

"You best get on home, Joseph," she said, calling him by his given name. "Tell your mama I'll be over to talk to her after supper."

Snooky took to his heels and bolted from the barn as if chased by a swarm of hornets. He knew serious trouble was on the way.

Supper was a grim and silent affair that evening. Walter and I were sent straight back to our rooms following the meal.

Later, Mama and Miss Dora had a long discussion and the upshot was that, for the next week, Walter, Snooky, and I were practically prisoners. We were forbidden to spend the night in our tent and Snooky could not come to visit unless Butch or Miss Dora walked over with him.

Mama kept me working with her, putting by the summer vegetables in Mason jars and washing windows.

Papa found plenty of chores for Walter too. Even when Snooky did visit, he was put to work with Walter painting, polishing brass, or mucking out stalls in the barn. Worst of all, Mama made me and Walter scrub and paint the "necessity."

The privy—or necessity, as Mama called it—was a two-seater with a lid over each chamber to discourage flies. It stood about two hundred feet behind the house at the edge of the outer dunes. This was inconvenient at night or when it rained, but necessary because of the smell. We planted sweet-smelling rosemary and horsemint around it, which didn't help much. Before you took a seat, you had to check carefully for scorpions as, for some reason, they find outhouses appealing.

Instead of paper on a roll, an old catalog or newspaper dangled from a rope between the seats. There was a little wooden keg of wood ashes on the floor with a scoop to sprinkle ashes over the contents of the privy chamber below the seats. The necessity was scrubbed weekly with lye soap and a hard brush.

Walter and I spent a miserable hot afternoon giving it an extra good wash and a coat of Papa's green Lighthouse Service paint.

The smell was so bad Walter tried to put a clothespin on his nose, but it wouldn't stay. Flies buzzed around us and the sweat trickled down my neck. I got paint on my coveralls and accidently dipped one braid in the bucket and then I got in trouble for that. All in all, it was one of my worst afternoons ever.

To make matters worse, Butch turned up to watch and laugh at us. He grabbed Walter's brush and brandished it like a sword, holding tight to my brother's arm. As Walter struggled to get loose, Butch painted a stripe across his coveralls.

"Don't!" said Walter. "You'll get me in trouble."

"I'll tell," I shouted.

"Better not," said Butch wickedly. "Tell your sister what happens to little girls who are tattletales," Butch told Walter.

"Don't tell," said Walter.

"But . . ." I began.

Just at that moment, Old Neb came shambling over the dunes and fairly trotted in our direction. Butch dropped the brush and released Walter's arm.

"Tell him to stay away," said Butch.

"Neb does what he wants," I said. "What are you so afraid of?"

"I ain't afraid. I'll deal with you two later," Butch said and took off running along the base of the dunes.

Old Neb stopped when he reached us and gave a snort. I reached up to hug his neck and gave him a kiss on the nose.

It seemed like we would never ever be set free again, let alone go looking for our treasure.

Chapter 7

FINALLY, as the last week of summer vacation began, Mama relented.

Each year, before we left for our winter house and school, she spent about a week putting things in order in the house on the island. She took everything off the pantry shelves and cleaned it thoroughly. Then she got out her sewing basket and mended the bed linens and all of Papa's clothes.

On Tuesday morning, I was finally released from forced labor and went to find Walter. He was working in the barn with Snooky, carrying manure from the stalls to the garden to be worked into the dirt. I was so happy not to be stringing beans or squeezing the slippery skins off scalding hot tomatoes that I picked up a pitchfork and set to work with them. Even the smell didn't bother me. We talked about the coming school year and friends we would see. After about an hour, Papa came into the barn to check on Walter and Snooky's progress and complimented us on our work.

"I see you have been hard at it and you've done a good job," he said. "Let's go and get some lunch."

Mama had set the table with a dish of cold smoked mullet, sliced tomatoes, thick slices of home-baked bread, and a plate of fresh churned butter.

We ate in silence until Papa said, "I believe these young'uns have turned over a new leaf, Mama. They've worked hard in the barn all morning."

Mama looked at him questioningly.

"I believe they deserve a reward," said Papa.

"What did you have in mind?" asked Mama.

"Y'all are leaving on Monday," said Papa. "I was going to have these youngsters take down the tent before they go and roll it up to store in the barn, but I believe we could let them have one more night in it before the summer is over."

"Oh, I don't know . . ." said Mama.

"Have you learned your lesson?" asked Papa.

Snooky, Walter, and I nodded eagerly. We hardly dared to breathe.

This was an unexpected turn of events and much better than we had thought possible.

"I don't know that Dora will allow it," said Mama, looking at Snooky.

"Let me talk to her," said Papa.

It was decided that we could spend the following night camping.

We were all on our best behavior. When suppertime rolled around, Walter and I carried our wienies and beans and our rolled-up blankets and pillows to the campsite. Snooky was already there with Butch building a campfire.

"You stick close to the tent," Butch warned us before he left. "Don't go wandering off and get lost, and watch out for panthers."

"Papa said there's no panthers on this island," I told him.

"Maybe he don't know everything," said Butch in a low scary voice.

"He knows more than you," I shot back.

"You best watch out who you talk to, girlie," said Butch, and he kind of slithered away into the gathering dark.

We cooked our wienies skewered on sticks and ate them wrapped in slices of Mama's bread with beans heated in the can on the open fire. Snooky had brought satsumas for our dessert. The moon was a thick crescent in a sky ablaze with stars. A brisk breeze blew in off the Gulf, keeping the mosquitoes at bay. We lay on our backs and watched for shooting stars until finally sleep overtook me.

The moon was high overhead and it must have been after midnight when something woke me. I sat up and looked at the remains of the fire, which was just ashes and coals. I looked around the campsite and realized I was alone.

Walter and Snooky must be in the tent, I thought and gathered up my blanket to join them but, when I pulled open the flap, I could see the cots were empty. Then I heard the faint sound of voices coming from the direction of the path to the bay. I knew immediately it was Walter and Snooky. I decided to see what they were up to, so I set off after the sound.

The moonlight filtering through the pines was barely bright enough to show me the path. I ran along the sandy trail as quietly as I could. Where were they going without me? I would show them I couldn't be left behind just because I was a girl.

I caught sight of Snooky and Walter just as I reached the cleared area around the Proctor house. They scuttled across the yard, keeping low and dodging from tree to shed to bush like Indians about to ambush a wagon train. They didn't know I was right behind them.

In the trees, a pair of owls was calling back and forth. Old Neb whinnied softly in his pole barn and stirred. I knew he could sense us but nothing else was moving in the house or the yard.

The boys were across the clearing and on the bay shore when I realized what they were after. The *Queen of the Sea* was beached there. Snooky and Walter were about to launch the boat for a midnight sail. Throwing caution to the wind, I dashed across the yard to join them.

"I'm going too," I hissed.

Walter gestured for me to be quiet. The three of us dragged the boat into the water and climbed aboard. Walter raised the sail and the fresh breeze from off the Gulf caught it and filled it at once. We were off. Nobody spoke again until we were away from the beach and gliding west across the bay.

"Where are you going? We need to go back," were the first words out of my mouth and I immediately regretted them.

"If you want to go back, swim," said Walter. "Me and Snooky are going treasure hunting!"

"Are you crazy?" I gasped.

"It's our last chance and we're gonna take it," said Walter.

"Our last chance," agreed Snooky and he held up the folding shovel and a burlap oyster bag for me to see.

They had planned this without me and come prepared.

"But you have never sailed to the end of the island," I argued. "What if we get lost?"

"How could we get lost?" asked Walter. "We can see the island. It's right there. We'll be able to see when we get to the end."

I had to admit this was true.

Away off to the south, lightning flashed.

The wind was picking up and the *Queen of the Sea* skimmed across the light chop. Walter was a good sailor. We had spent hours sailing on the bay, although never this far from home.

It's amazing how fast a squall can come up on you in the summertime.

We had been running parallel to the shore for about twenty minutes and were well along. I forgot to be worried because I was enjoying the ride. The island looked beautiful silhouetted against distant lightning, and thunder rumbled faintly. Suddenly, the world grew darker. I looked around and realized that clouds were stealing rapidly across the sky and eating up the stars. The moon had just been consumed and the wind was kicking up. I tugged at Walter's shirt and pointed but he ignored me.

"Walter, it's a storm," I shouted, tugging his sleeve.

He brushed off my hand.

"We're almost there," he replied.

"We need to go back," I insisted.

"We're too far," he shot back.

Suddenly lightning split the sky and the waves began to kick up fast.

"We need to go back," I pleaded.

Big raindrops began to fall and although we couldn't see them, we felt them slap our faces. Snooky looked scared.

Walter was struggling to keep the boat steady as the wind grew fierce and the waves threatened to swamp us. I had to hold hard to the edge of the boat to keep from tumbling out. Water streamed down our faces.

Walter turned the little boat hard and I realized he was heading for the shore.

Waves broke over the *Queen*'s bow and Walter had to tack back and forth, running at an angle, to make any progress. I began to bail with my hands and Snooky followed my lead. With the boat nearly swamped, we ran aground about twelve feet offshore and struggled through the breaking surf for high ground. Walter tried to hold onto the bowline and drag the *Queen* to safety but it soon became clear we could barely save ourselves. Although the water was only knee deep, it was a struggle just to remain standing as the waves rolled in higher and higher.

We made for the cover of some twisted oak trees that provided a little protection from the wind and torrents of rain and huddled together while lightning flashed like Fourth of July fireworks.

We watched the *Queen of the Sea* sail away without us and then capsize. We were on the bay side of the island miles from home and with no transportation. Gradually the rain became less violent.

"We need to start back," I said. "Mama and Papa will be worried."

Walter nodded and the three of us began slogging our way east. Although the wind had calmed a bit, the pounding surf made walking along the beach impossible in most places. We struggled along the edge of the interior jungle with briar vines slashing at our legs until we came to a point where runoff from the rain had created a temporary creek. The ground was already completely saturated from rain earlier in the week and a flood gushed into the bay in front of us, cascading between the dripping foliage and sodden dunes. The stream was ten feet wide but how deep was a mystery. It was still raining at that point and we wore only shorts and T-shirts. I was soaked to the skin and starting to wonder if we would ever get back.

Walter waded into the flood a little ways, holding his arms out for balance and placing his feet carefully.

"Come on! It's not deep," he urged. He took two more steps and plunged into water up to his waist without warning. Then we were all screaming and he was struggling to hold on to the thorny stalk of a frond on a low scrub palm.

I saw a big shadowy form approaching along the beach moving not rapidly but steadily in our direction. By the time the creature reached the floodwater, I could see it was Old Neb. Without hesitation, he waded into the flood and went to my brother, who was able to grab him and mount the horse, who carried him back to where we stood. Old Neb plodded through the rushing water and, when he reached the sand, Walter slid from his back.

Snooky and I hugged Walter and then we hugged Neb.

Neb nuzzled us and snorted, then he turned in the direction he had come from and stood as if waiting for something. Walter grabbed his mane and scrambled onto his back, Snooky climbed up behind him and I climbed up in front.

When we were settled, Neb waded back into the creek, which was no deterrent to his great bulk, and started for home at his slow steady pace. It was nearly dawn when we reached the Proctor house. The rain had stopped and sunrise was painting the black clouds with liquid gold.

Miss Dora was ecstatic when she heard us scramble up onto the porch calling for her. She came running out to hug us and then to scold us in no uncertain terms with tears streaming down her pale cheeks.

We had already been missed. Papa had seen the storm coming and went to the tent to bring us in before it broke. He found the tent empty and went looking for us. He and Butch were now searching the island on horseback. Miss Dora bundled us inside and gave us dry clothes and blankets. She fetched a shotgun from the closet and, standing on the porch, fired it three times to signal to the searchers. She gave us hot milk and demanded to know where we had been.

Dooly and Honey were hugging her skirts crying when Papa and Butch arrived half an hour later.

Papa hugged us and kissed us and then, after he had brought us home to Mama and she had hugged us and kissed us, I got spanked for the first and only time I can remember.

We spent our last summer days on St. George that year confined to the porch.

After we returned to the mainland, news of our exploit spread fast. At school, we were overwhelmed with questions about our adventure. Mama forbade us to bring the chain to school for show-and-tell. She said the attention would only encourage our bad behavior. Even so, we were celebrities for a time.

Our punishment continued for the entire month of September. We came straight home after school, ate supper, did our homework, and went to bed.

By Christmas, Walter and I had been pardoned, which was a relief because we had both been concerned about how Santa would view our illicit treasure hunt. We spent Christmas with Papa on the island, but the tent was not pitched again until late the following July.

In my stocking, I found the best gift of all—my gold coin strung on a fine gold chain. Butch had returned it to Papa after the night of our adventure. After Walter and I fought, he and Snooky had taken it from my drawer hoping to impress Butch. He had taken it away from the younger boys. It was Butch who had wrecked Mama's oyster bar hoping to find more gold.

Of course, there was no treasure. Butch had made the map and left it for us to find as a joke, just as he had been the panther, stolen the skillet, and done a dozen other mean little tricks because he was lonely and bored. He admitted everything to Papa the night of the search.

He had also watched us as we searched, planning to confiscate any real valuables we might find.

The *Queen of the Sea* washed ashore at the west end as if she completed our journey on her own. Her mast was broken and there was some damage to her hull, but Papa towed her home and worked on her over the winter. She was shipshape by our next summer vacation.

I still wear my coin around my neck. As to the silver chain, maybe it is from a treasure ship. I don't know. But there really were pirates on St. George Island once upon a time.

Here are some other books from Pineapple Press that might interest you.

For a complete catalog, write to Pineapple Press, P.O. Box 3889, Sarasota, Florida 34230-3889, or call (800) 746-3275. Or visit our website at *www.pineapplepress.com*.

El Lector by William Durbin. In 1931 in Ybor City, Florida, Bella wants to be a lector just like her grandfather, who reads to cigar workers. But the Depression makes it seem impossible. Ages 9–12.

Olivia Brophie and the Pearl of Tagelus by Chris Tozier. Fantasy fiction. Olivia Brophie's dad has sent her to live with her eccentric aunt and uncle in the Florida scrub. Life is boring until bears follow her to school and tree frogs start writing cryptic messages on her bedroom window. Olivia slips down a tortoise burrow into the vast Floridan aquifer, where ancient animals thrive in a mysterious world. Age 8 and up.

Olivia Brophie and the Sky Island by Chris Tozier. Second book in the Olivia Brophie series. Olivia's life is in turmoil ever since she accidentally froze all of the earth's water and her aunt and uncle were kidnapped by the Wardenclyffe thugs. With the help of a black bear named Hoolie, she must travel across America to undo the damage she caused. Meanwhile, Doug and Gnat are drawn deeper into the world of Junonia, the mysterious city beneath the Floridan aquifer. Age 8 and up.

A Land Remembered, Student Edition, by Patrick Smith. Florida's favorite historical novel in a two-volume edition for young readers. Volume 1 covers the first generation of MacIveys to arrive in Florida and Zech's coming of age. Volume 2 covers Zech's son, Solomon, and the exploitation of the land as his own generation prospers. Age 9 and up.

The Spy Who Came In from the Sea by Peggy Nolan. Fourteen-year-old Frank Hollahan moves to Jacksonville, Florida, in 1943. When he reports that he saw a spy land on the local beach and no one believes him, he sets out to prove the spy's existence. Ages 8–14.

Blood Moon Rider by Zack Waters. Young Harley Wallace is sent to live with his grandfather in Florida during World War II. He and his new friend, Beth, embark on an adventure involving murder, a disappearance, and German U-boats lurking in the Gulf of Mexico.

Solomon by Marilyn Bishop Shaw. Florida Historical Society Award for Best Youth-Oriented Book. Eleven-year-old Solomon and his parents, newly freed slaves, work to build a Florida homestead. Ages 9–14.

Kidnapped in Key West by Edwina Raffa and Annelle Rigsby. It's 1912 and 12-year-old Eddie's father has been falsely accused of a crime in Key West. When Eddie comes to his rescue, he's kidnapped! Ages 8–12.

Escape to the Everglades by Edwina Raffa and Annelle Rigsby. Running Boy's mother was Seminole, his father white. Now 14, he has received his adult name and hopes to prove his loyalty to the Snake Clan by joining Osceola's warriors during the Second Seminole War. Ages 9–12.

The Treasure of Amelia Island by M.C. Finotti. Winner of the Florida Historical Society's Horgan Award. Eleven-year-old Mary Kingsley, daughter of historical figure Ana Jai Kingsley, tells the tumultuous events of 1813 when the Patriots try to force Spain out of La Florida. Amidst all this, Mary and her brothers search for pirate treasure. Includes a reader's guide. Ages 8–12.

Ponce de Leon and the Discovery of Florida by Sandra Wallus Sammons. In 1513 Juan Ponce de Leon sailed into the unknown to discover new lands. He stopped at one place that seemed to be an island but that was really part of a whole new continent. He named it "La Florida." Ages 9–12.

Zore Neale Hurston: Wrapped in Rainbows by Sandra Wallus Sammons. Zora Neale Hurston carefully collected the folklore of African-Americans living in Florida by listening to their tales and writing down what they said. She wrote several books that have earned her a place in American literature. Ages 9–12.

Marjory Stoneman Douglas and the Florida Everglades by Sandra Wallus Sammons. Called the "grandmother of the Everglades," Marjory Stoneman Douglas was a tireless crusader for the preservation of the famed River of Grass. Read about her childhood up North and her long and inspiring life in Florida. Ages 9–12.

Marjorie Kinnan Rawlings and the Florida Crackers by Sandra Wallus Sammons. Marjorie Kinnan Rawlings grew up hoping to become an author. When she moved to Florida, she met the so-called Crackers and wrote stories about them. Her novel *The Yearling* won the Pulitzer Prize for fiction. Ages 9–12.

The Two Henrys by Sandra Wallus Sammons. Henry Flagler and Henry Plant changed the landscape of Florida in the late 1800s and early 1900s. This dual biography is the story of railroads and the men who built them. Flagler opened up Florida's east coast with his railroads and hotels, and Plant did the same on the west coast. Age 12 and up.

Henry Flagler, Builder of Florida by Sandra Wallus Sammons. An exciting biography about the man who changed Florida's east coast. Already a millionaire when he first visited Florida in 1878, Henry Flagler later returned and built railroads and hotels to open up the coast to visitors. By 1912 he had built a railroad all the way to Key West. Ages 9–12.

Those Amazing Animals series. Each book in this series includes 20 questions and answers about an animal, 20 photos, and 20 funny illustrations. Learn about alligators, bears, flamingos, turtles, vultures, and many more. Ages 5–9.

Iguana Invasion! Exotic Pets Gone Wild in Florida by Virginia Aronson and Allyn Szejko. Green iguanas, Burmese pythons, Nile monitor lizards, rhesus monkeys, and many more non-native animals are rapidly increasing in population in subtropical Florida. This full-color book provides scientific information, exciting wildlife stories, and photos for the most common exotic animals on the loose, most of them offspring of abandoned pets. Age 12 and up.

The Gopher Tortoise by Ray and Patricia Ashton. Explains the critical role this tortoise and its burrow play in the upland ecosystem of Florida and the Southeast. Learn how scientists study this animal and try to protect it. Age 10 and up.

My Florida Facts by Russell and Annie Johnson. Learn facts about Florida, from the state capital to the number of counties, from what states border Florida to how to make a Key lime pie. A kid-friendly book that makes learning fun by singing along with the "My Florida Facts" song, included on a CD. Ages 8–12.

The Crafts of Florida's First People by Robin Brown. Learn how the earliest Indians got their food, made clothing, and cooked meals by doing these things the way they did, using materials you can find in Florida today. Includes illustrated instructions on how to make pottery, weave cloth, build traps, start a fire without matches, and more. Age 10 and up.

America's REAL First Thanksgiving by Robyn Gioia. When most Americans think of the first Thanksgiving, they think of the Pilgrims and the Indians in New England in 1621. But on September 8, 1565, the Spanish and the native Timucua celebrated with a feast of Thanksgiving in St. Augustine. Teacher's activity guide also available. Ages 9–14.

CPSIA information can be obtained at www.ICGtesting.com
Printed in the USA
BVOW08s1047140415

396010BV00007B/15/P